~⊱ BOOK NINE ⊰~

SOLTRA
THE STONE CHARMER

→ BOOK NINE ←

SOLTRA
THE STONE CHARMER

ADAM BLADE
ILLUSTRATED BY EZRA TUCKER

SCHOLASTIC INC.

New York Toronto London Auckland Sydney
Mexico City New Delhi Hong Kong Buenos Aires

With special thanks to Allan Frewin

For Karen

No part of this work may be reproduced, stored in a retrieval system, or transmitted in any form or by any means, electronic, mechanical, photocopying, recording, or otherwise, without written permission of the publisher. For information regarding permission, write to Working Partners Ltd., Stanley House, St. Chad's Place, London WC1X 9HH, United Kingdom.

ISBN-13: 978-0-545-06865-9
ISBN-10: 0-545-06865-7

Beast Quest series created by Working Partners Ltd., London. BEAST QUEST is a trademark of Working Partners Ltd.

Copyright © 2008 by Working Partners Ltd.

All rights reserved. Published by Scholastic Inc., 557 Broadway, New York, NY 10012, by arrangement with Working Partners Ltd.

SCHOLASTIC, LITTLE APPLE, and associated logos are trademarks and/or registered trademarks of Scholastic Inc.

12 11 10 9 8 7 6 5 4 3 2   8 9 10 11 12 13/0

Designed by Tim Hall
Printed in the U.S.A.
First printing, December 2008

Did you think it was over?

Did you think I would accept defeat and disappear?

No! That can never be. I am Malvel, the Dark Wizard who strikes fear into the hearts of the people of Avantia. I still have much more to show this wretched kingdom, and one boy in particular — Tom.

The young hero liberated the six Beasts of Avantia from my curse. But his fight is far from over. Let us see how he fares with a new Quest, one that will surely crush him and his companion, Elenna.

Avantia's Beasts had good hearts that I corrupted for my own wicked purpose. Now, thanks to Tom, they are free to protect the kingdom once more. But I have created new supreme Beasts whose hearts are evil and so cannot be set free. Each one guards a piece of the most precious relic of Avantia, a relic I have stolen: the suit of golden armor that gives magical strength to its rightful owner. I will stop at nothing to prevent Tom from collecting the complete suit and defeating me again. This time he will not win!

Malvel

IT HAD BEEN A LONG DAY FOR FARMER GRETLIN. He plodded along the earth furrows behind his two oxen. Sweat dripped down his neck as he guided the heavy plow through the soil.

The sun was setting over the marsh that lay to the west of the farm. The farmer looked up, then frowned, lifting an arm to mop his brow. Dense fog was beginning to creep from the marsh across the field. It was unusual for it to be so thick at this time of year.

Shivering a little, he unharnessed the oxen and began to lead them toward the stable. The animals were usually eager for their meal at day's end, but now the farmer could hardly get them to move. He snapped the leather harness, then frowned again. The harness had become icy cold in his fingers. He turned. The two oxen had come to a dead halt.

"What's wrong, lads?" he asked, walking back to them. Tendrils of fog encircled them all, cutting them off from the farmhouse. He patted the neck of one ox, then let out a shocked gasp. Instead of warm flesh, his hand had touched a hard, cold surface.

The two animals had turned to stone!

As he looked into the oxen's great brown eyes — which were still moving, wide and rolling with fear — he saw a shadowy, milky outline reflected in them.

Something or someone was standing right behind him.

He turned, crying out in fear as he stared at the female figure that had stepped from the heart of the fog. The setting sun shone behind her, ringing her with a golden glow.

The woman was two heads taller than he, her body swathed in a shining, rippling garment — like a cloak made of black water. He gazed up into the woman's face — but found that she *had* no face, just a featureless surface, marble smooth and milky white.

Then the final terror came.

The creature's face folded up on itself like a huge eyelid — and from beneath that eyelid stared a single great eye, as green and clear as an emerald.

Gretlin stared into the unblinking eye and suddenly his fear slipped away.

He took a step toward the woman, close enough now for him to see his own reflection in the great green eye. Crystals of ice filled his veins, deadening his limbs and freezing his heart.

Moments later, like his oxen, only his eyes could move. His body was encased in stone.

The woman turned, her cloak undulating as she drifted back into the fog.

A few moments later, Farmer Gretlin saw a movement out of the corner of his eye. A small boy was crouching in terror behind the low drystone wall that marked the boundary of the field. He tried to call to the boy, to ask him to fetch help, but the only sound that escaped him was a groan.

Terrified, the boy ran toward the village.

The fog curled around the farmer's shoulders like a shroud.

How long would it be before death took him?

↦ CHAPTER ONE ↤

HOMEWARD BOUND

A_T LAST!" GASPED TOM. HE HAD PUSHED past a tangle of dense undergrowth and branches to find himself gazing out over open countryside.

"No kidding!" said Elenna, close behind him. "I was beginning to think the Dark Jungle went on forever."

They stepped out into the cool of the late afternoon, exhausted and glad to be free of the dark, sultry heat.

Ahead of them, the land sloped downward in grassy terraces to a wide, winding river that rushed through deep, stony banks.

Tom took one final glance back into the sinister

jungle, thinking of his battle with Claw the Giant Ape, and remembering how he had just managed to snatch the golden chain mail from the evil Beast.

Silver the wolf and Storm, Tom's noble stallion, emerged from the jungle, too. Silver bounded and barked joyfully, and Storm neighed and pranced.

"They're glad to be out in the open," Elenna said. "Can we camp for the night down by the river? I could catch us some fish for supper."

Tom sighed, looking into the distance.

"What's wrong?" she asked.

"I was thinking about Aduro," he replied. "I'm worried about what Malvel might have done to him."

The Dark Wizard Malvel had kidnapped their friend and protector, Wizard Aduro. Malvel had appeared to them in a vision after Tom's defeat of Claw, showing them torn strips of Aduro's red cloak. Was the good wizard even still alive?

Whatever fate had befallen Aduro, Tom knew that he had to fulfill his Quest and unite the six parts of the golden armor that Malvel had stolen and scattered across the kingdom. Aduro had told them it was the only way they could rescue him. Only then would the land of Avantia be safe from the six evil Beasts Malvel had set loose.

The friends and their two animal companions made their way to the river. They followed it through the valley, down to a rocky beach.

Tom watched as Elenna waded into the water with an arrow on her bow. After a long wait, she fired the arrow and a moment later was splashing her way up to the shore with a large salmon. She left it on a rock and went back to catch some more.

Silver sniffed the fish but shook his big, shaggy head and trotted off. Tom guessed that he was on the prowl for something he'd find a bit tastier. Storm was grazing contentedly on some tall grass.

Tom felt tired and homesick as he looked at the racing river, thinking how different it was from the wide, still lake beside his home village of Errinel. He had not seen it for a long time now.

He shook himself and started to gather wood for a fire. He made two tripods of sturdy twigs and skewered the salmon on another twig to hang above the flames. By the time Elenna returned with more fish, the fire was ready.

The twilight deepened as the fish cooked, and as they ate, Tom told Elenna about his home. "The lake is as clear as crystal," he said. "On hot summer evenings everyone goes to the lakeshore to eat, play music, and watch the sunset."

"It sounds lovely," Elenna said through a mouthful of salmon.

"People say that the water has healing properties," Tom continued, gazing at the darkening sky. "The water has to be collected as the sun sets." He laughed. "It's just a legend," he said. "I don't suppose it's true."

"It's a nice story, all the same," Elenna said. "And after all that we've seen, who knows what's true and what isn't? Most people think the Beasts are a myth, but we know they're not."

After they had finished their meal, Tom and Elenna went to check on their companions. Silver was lying with his head between his paws, snoring softly. Storm stood close by, dozing peacefully.

The two friends found a place to spread their bedrolls for the night. Tom kept the pieces of armor that he had already recovered by his side. The golden helmet, forged into the shape of an eagle's head, gleamed softly in the growing starlight. He reached out and touched the chain mail vest, wondering about the Master of the Beasts who had worn it before him. He thought of his own father, Taladon the Swift, who had undertaken a Beast Quest of his own many years ago, but had disappeared. *I wish I had known him,* he thought drowsily. He hoped they might be reunited one day.

The next day dawned bright and warm, the sun rising in a clear blue sky. Tom unrolled the magical map of Avantia, which Aduro had given him when his adventures first began.

As he studied it, the map came to life. Meadow grass moved in the wind and the tiny mountains were cold to the touch. The forests and rivers, villages and castles were all miniature versions of the real landscape of Avantia.

A glowing red path usually appeared on the map, showing Tom where to find his next challenge, but for the moment there was no sign of it.

"There!" exclaimed Elenna after they had been staring at the map for a little while.

A tiny heart of golden light was glowing on the

map. As Tom and Elenna peered, it pulsed and grew larger until they could make out the shape of a golden breastplate.

"It's the next piece of armor!" Elenna said.

Tom let out a cry of delight. "Yes!" he gasped. "And look where it is." He pointed to a wide, clear lake set in rich farmlands. Beside the lake nestled a small village. "It's Errinel, my home. You'll be able to meet Uncle Henry and Aunt Maria, who brought me up." Tom felt his eyes fill with tears. "I haven't seen them since I started the Quest," he said.

A large muzzle snuffled close to his ear. It was Silver, his eyes bright with understanding. Tom turned with a grin. Storm was close by, pawing at the shingle with a hoof.

"You can't hide your feelings from us," Elenna said with a laugh. "We know how much you want to go home. Come on — let's pack up camp and get going."

"Yes!" Tom laughed. "And no stopping till we get to Errinel!"

But his laughter soon faded as he thought of his Quest and of the dangers that lay ahead. He had to get to Errinel quickly — but what kind of Beast would be waiting there for them?

And what harm had it already done to his home and his family?

CHAPTER TWO

TURNED TO STONE

TOM AND ELENNA SAT ASTRIDE STORM'S BROAD back as he cantered along, with Silver loping at his side. Despite the perils that lay ahead, Tom was glad to be heading home. It had been an easy journey so far, following the weaving line of the river. The day was hot, but a fresh breeze kept them cool. Brightly colored butterflies and jeweled dragonflies danced over the water.

"We're nearly there," Tom said at last. A thrill of excitement shot through him at the thought of seeing his uncle and aunt again. But this would be no ordinary homecoming. The image of a golden breastplate had brought him here, and that could only mean one of Malvel's evil Beasts was lurking near the village.

"We should leave the river now and go up over that low hill," Tom said, pointing. "There's a small wood on the other side, and then it's all farmland till we get to Errinel."

They rode up the gentle slope of the hill and down into the woods.

Silver trotted beside them, sniffing the air as if he were trying to pick up a scent.

"What is it, boy?" Elenna asked. "Can you smell something?"

The wolf let out a soft whine. Storm whickered and turned his head. Something was unsettling the animals.

Tom's hand went to his sword hilt. His shield, which carried six magical tokens from the good Beasts of Avantia, was slung over his shoulder. He had freed all the Beasts from Malvel's evil curse — Ferno the Fire Dragon, Sepron the Sea Serpent,

Cypher the Mountain Giant, Tagus the Night Horse, Tartok the Ice Beast, and Epos the Winged Flame — and he knew he could call on them if he was in trouble. The golden chain mail and helmet he had already retrieved from Zepha the Monster Squid and Claw the Giant Ape were close at hand in the saddlebag. The chain mail gave him strength of heart and the helmet sharpened his sight. His powers were growing with every Quest. He was ready for battle.

"I think there's danger nearby," he murmured.

Elenna nodded, sliding an arrow from her quiver and slotting it into the bowstring.

Slowly they came out of the woods and made their way along a track between high hedges. Through gaps in the hedgerows, they could see fields all around them and the occasional distant farmhouse or barn.

"It all seems normal enough," Tom said warily. "Except . . ." He frowned. There was something wrong, but he couldn't put his finger on it. And then it struck him. "It's too quiet. What has happened to all the birds?"

"There's a row of starlings over there," Elenna said, pointing to a wooden gate ahead of them.

Tom peered at the birds as they approached. He expected them to take fright and flap away over the fields. But they didn't move. The hair prickled on the back of his neck.

Tom slid down from the saddle and walked up to the birds, then let out a breath as he realized they were just statues. He reached out to touch one of them. The bird's body was hard and cold.

"They aren't real," he called back. "They're made of stone."

Elenna jumped down and ran over to his side. She touched one of the small statues, then leaned in closer. "You can see every tiny detail of the feathers," she said. "They are too perfect to have been carved. Tom, I don't like this."

Then Tom spotted something in the field beyond — a gray-brown shape in the stubble of newly cropped hay.

He climbed the gate and walked over to the shape, crouching down beside it and reaching out a hand. It was a stone hare, its long limbs stretched as if it had been frozen in mid-flight. Tom picked it up and carried it back to the gate. He laid it at the roadside and stared down at it with a frown.

Silver moved hesitantly toward the hare and sniffed it. A moment later, he bounded away, snorting and shaking his muzzle.

Elenna shivered. "What are you thinking?" she asked Tom.

He looked at her. "I don't believe they're statues at all," he said. "I think something has turned living creatures into stone."

"It must be Malvel's evil Beast," Elenna murmured.

A new urgency filled Tom's heart. "We have to

get to the village," he said. "Let's hope the Beast hasn't been there yet." The thought of his aunt and uncle and the other villagers of Errinel turned to stone was too awful.

The two friends jumped back into Storm's saddle.

Tom pressed his heels into the stallion's sides and the horse broke into a gallop. Silver ran close by, his body low to the ground.

The village was a few miles away through the fields. Tom remembered the fragment of a horseshoe given to him by Tagus the Night Horse. It had the power to give him great speed.

He touched the magical token in his shield and Storm began to gallop faster than Tom had ever known. He clung to Storm's back as the stallion flew through the fields, and Elenna gripped Tom's belt as the wind whistled past their ears. Silver bounded alongside the racing horse, his tongue lolling.

A few moments later, Tom saw something strange ahead of them in a nearby field.

"Stop!" he called.

Storm came to a halt. Tom jumped down and ran toward a low fence.

"I know this field," he called to Elenna as she leaped off the stallion's back. "It belongs to Farmer Gretlin. Look!" He pointed a shaking finger over the fence.

Three gray figures stood unmoving in the newly plowed field: a team of oxen and a man. All had been turned to stone.

⇥ Chapter Three ⇤

A Sword to the Heart

TOM STOOD ON THE BOTTOM BAR OF THE FENCE and stared out across the desolate field.

"The Beast could still be nearby," he said worriedly. "And it could turn *us* into stone!" He strode back toward Storm. "I have to be prepared for anything."

He slipped on the heavy chain mail and pulled on the golden helmet. Now he would feel no fear and be able to see the Beast if it was still lurking. He climbed back into the saddle, slipping his shield over his left arm and loosening his sword in its scabbard.

Elenna scrambled up behind him, her bow drawn and her quiver of arrows at hand.

"Go, boy!" Tom said to Storm, nudging with his heels. The stallion backed away from the fence, then, with a surge of power, leaped forward and took the fence in one long, smooth jump.

Fearlessly, Storm cantered toward the frozen stone figures, the ever-loyal Silver by his side. Tom expected an attack from the Beast, but they crossed the field without harm. The two animals were uneasy, though, as if they sensed that danger was close at hand.

Everything was eerily silent as they came to a stop near the stone figures. Tom and Elenna slid down from the saddle. Storm neighed nervously and backed away. Silver circled the man and his oxen, sniffing the air, his ears down and the hair along his back as stiff as wire.

"It's Farmer Gretlin!" Tom cried as he and Elenna drew near. Cautiously, he reached out and touched the stone man's chest. It was cold.

Elenna frowned. "He looks happy," she said, as she gazed into the farmer's face. "I don't understand. Why would someone who is about to be turned to stone be so happy?"

"Malvel's Beasts are usually terrifying," Tom said, confused. "This must have been done by something that looks harmless, but isn't."

"Something beautiful, even," added Elenna.

"Beautiful and deadly," Tom said grimly. "This is bad, Elenna. How do you fight something that doesn't seem dangerous?"

"What do you think the Beast looks like?" asked Elenna.

Tom gazed sadly into the farmer's face. "The only person who could tell us has been killed," he murmured. But then he looked closer, staring up into the farmer's eyes. Was it his imagination or had he seen a movement?

"Elenna," Tom said urgently, "I think he's alive."

His friend looked carefully. "You could be right," she said. As she moved closer, her elbow struck the statue. It made a curiously hollow sound.

Tom rapped his knuckles against the statue's arm. Again, they heard the hollow sound.

"The stone is just a shell around him," Tom cried.

"But how can we break the shell without hurting him?" Elenna asked.

Tom drew his sword.

"You can't!" Elenna gasped. "You'll kill him."

"Not if I find the weak point," Tom said. "My uncle is a blacksmith, remember? He taught me always to search for the weak spot, and then to use it." He circled the farmer. "There has to be a crack or a fault line somewhere," he muttered. "There *has* to be!"

Suddenly, he noticed a hairline crack in the man's chest — just above the heart.

"There!" he said. He lifted his sword and carefully placed the lethal tip against the crack.

"No!" Elenna cried out. "It's too dangerous. If you slip — if you make one wrong move — the blade will go into his heart."

"I won't slip," Tom said. "And we have no choice. We can't leave him like this, and we need him to tell us about the Beast."

"Be careful," Elenna whispered, stepping back as Tom readied himself for the blow. But he felt very sure of himself, and the golden helmet gave him perfect vision as he guided the point of his sword toward the crack.

He twisted the sword and pushed the blade into the stone.

Nothing happened. Frowning, Tom drew back his hand and slammed his palm hard against the hilt of the sword. He heard Elenna give a gasp of alarm. Storm and Silver were watching with worried eyes.

He struck the hilt a second time. The stone rang — but the crack held.

This was no time to give up. Tom hit the hilt a third time. He saw the crack widen. A web of fractures spun out across the farmer's chest and down his limbs.

Then the stone shell shattered into fragments and tumbled to the ground.

Farmer Gretlin's chest gave a great heave as he sucked air into his lungs and fell forward onto his hands and knees, gasping and coughing.

He was alive!

CHAPTER FOUR

INTO THE WOODS

TOM TOOK A WATER BOTTLE FROM STORM'S saddlebag and bent down to give it to the gasping farmer. As he drank, Elenna stood over him, arrow at the ready, eyes scanning the empty field.

"Who are you?" Farmer Gretlin gasped.

Tom took off his helmet and grinned.

"Tom!" exclaimed the farmer. "You've saved my life! Help me up." He put a hand on Tom's shoulder and got shakily to his feet.

"What did this to you?" Elenna asked.

The farmer gave her a curious look. "And who are *you*?"

"She's my friend, Elenna," Tom said. "We're here to help. Can you tell us what happened?"

The farmer's eyes narrowed. "There was fog over the marsh," he said. "And a tall lady dressed in black." A shudder went through him. "She had no face, just a huge green eye. It was the most beautiful eye I've ever seen. And then I couldn't move." He smiled gratefully at them. "Until you came to my aid."

"How long ago was this?" Tom asked.

The farmer shook his head. "A day," he said uncertainly. "Maybe more."

"Who can this woman be?" Tom wondered aloud, as the farmer and Elenna went to check on the stone oxen.

His heart began to race as a familiar, cruel voice whispered in his ear, "Would you like to meet Soltra the Stone Charmer face-to-face?"

"Malvel!" Tom spun around, but saw

nothing. "I'm not afraid of you, or any of your evil Beasts."

The Dark Wizard let out a laugh like the hissing of snakes. "There is no victory for you here, boy. Soltra cannot be beaten."

"I'll beat her!" Tom snarled. "You'll see!"

But there was no reply — the voice was gone.

Tom gripped his sword, wishing he could put the cold steel into Malvel's wicked heart.

"The Beast is called Soltra," he said to Elenna when she came back. He looked over to Farmer Gretlin, who was still checking the stone oxen. "Malvel just spoke to me. He says she can't be beaten."

"I don't believe that," Elenna said. "We'll find a way!"

Tom nodded. "You're right. We should go to the village — and let's hope she hasn't already been there." What if his aunt and uncle had already fallen victim to Soltra? He tried not to think about it.

They walked back to Gretlin, Storm and Silver following with wide, watchful eyes.

"Can you bring these creatures back to life?" Farmer Gretlin asked.

Tom stared carefully at the two animals. There didn't seem to be any sign of life in the stony eyes. He shook his head regretfully. "I'm sorry," he said.

Tom and Elenna helped the farmer across the plowed field, then walked along the winding road that led to the village. Tom gazed around, memories flooding back, as the familiar rooftops and chimneys of Errinel came into sight above the trees.

The village was silent and deserted, save for three gray statues: one woman carrying a woven basket; another laying out wares on a market stall; and a man with his arm lifted, as if he were trying to shield his eyes from the sun. Soltra had been here.

A lump filled Tom's throat. He remembered the village square as a place filled with noise and bustle as the cheerful people of Errinel went about their daily lives, not this empty, desolate silence. He examined the three statues but could not find a single crack to help him break their stone prisons. Farmer Gretlin had been lucky.

An urgent fear built inside Tom as he ran from house to house, hoping desperately to find someone who had managed to survive Soltra's enchantment. But there was no one.

"The rest of the villagers must have fled," Gretlin said.

They came to the forge where Tom's uncle Henry worked. The familiar bellows lay beside the fire, and the ironworking tools were set out on the worktable as usual.

"Where has everyone gone?" asked Farmer Gretlin. "How are we to find them?"

Tom gave a grim smile. "We have a wolf, don't

we?" he said. He called to Silver, and the wolf padded into the forge and looked questioningly up at him. Tom took an old leather apron down from a peg on the wall. "Here, Silver," he said. "This will have Uncle Henry's scent."

Silver sniffed at the apron. A moment later, he let out a sharp bark and ran from the forge.

"Follow him!" Tom cried. "He's got the scent!"

Silver glided along, his body low, his muzzle to the ground, moving fast but stopping every now and then to allow the others to catch up. Soon he was leading them toward dense woodland on the other side of the town.

Tom turned to Farmer Gretlin. "Will you stay in the village in case anyone comes back?" he asked. "And keep Storm with you?"

"I will," said the farmer. "Good luck."

Leaving Storm and Gretlin, Tom and Elenna followed Silver. They pushed their way through brambles and ferns, keeping the speeding wolf in sight as they plunged deeper and deeper into the woods.

Soon they came to a dell filled with a tangle of ivy and briars. There was no sign of Silver. A few moments later, a sharp bark broke the silence. Tom turned and ran toward the sound, but he had only gone a few steps when his foot caught in a snarl of ivy roots. He sprawled headlong.

"Tom! Are you all right?" called a familiar voice.

Tom struggled to his feet as Aunt Maria emerged from the cover of the trees, her face filled with joy and concern. And right behind her was Uncle Henry.

They were safe!

↦ CHAPTER FIVE ↤

REUNION

TOM WAS CAUGHT UP IN A HUGE BEAR HUG BY his aunt and uncle, and for a few moments he forgot all about the danger they faced.

"How many of you escaped?" he asked.

Villagers stepped out of cover and stood uneasily around him, their faces pale and anxious.

"We're all safe," said Uncle Henry. "All those who ran." He frowned at Tom. "But how did you know what had happened?"

Tom looked thoughtfully at his uncle and aunt and the gathered villagers. Aduro had always told him not to talk to the ordinary folk of Avantia about the Beasts, but people of Errinel had been turned to stone by Soltra — and they deserved to know what she was.

He raised his voice so that everyone would be able to hear him. "What I'm going to tell you is the deepest secret in all Avantia, and no one must ever speak of it outside the village," he told them. "I am under the guidance of Wizard Aduro, adviser to King Hugo. I have come here with my friends, Elenna, Storm, and Silver, to find the Stone Charmer, an evil Beast."

There was a murmur of amazement.

Uncle Henry stepped forward. "You are the true son of your father," he said solemnly. "And I see from your face, and from the weapons and armor you bear, that you are ready for your challenge. Tell us what we should do."

It made Tom feel proud that Uncle Henry knew he could be trusted with such an important task.

"Soltra seems to have left the village for now," he said. "We should go back there for rest and food. If I am to defeat her, I need to know everything that happened in Errinel."

When they returned to the blacksmith's house, Aunt Maria warmed up a stew she had made, while Uncle Henry told Tom and Elenna how a village boy had seen Soltra with Farmer Gretlin at sunset, and had run to warn the others.

"That is how most of us managed to escape before the Beast came," Aunt Maria said as she ladled the hearty stew into wooden bowls for Tom and Elenna.

"So Soltra appeared at sunset last night," Tom said. "She must not be able to survive in full daylight. That's her one weakness."

"It's already late afternoon," Elenna pointed out. "The sun will be setting soon."

"I know," Tom said. "So we don't have much

time." He looked at his uncle. "We should lead the villagers to the shores of the lake for safety."

"The lake?" Uncle Henry said in a puzzled voice. "But if she comes to us there, we'll have deep water at our backs. How will we escape then?"

"The old tales say the water has healing powers," Tom said. "Perhaps it will be enough to save the people of Errinel."

Elenna looked curiously at him and leaned to whisper in his ear, "I thought you didn't believe in that story."

"I'm prepared to believe in *anything* right now," he murmured.

"But shouldn't we find the Beast right away?" Elenna asked.

"We will," Tom said firmly. "But not before the villagers are all taken to safety. We'll spend the night at the lake — then we'll find Soltra when the sun comes up tomorrow. She'll be more vulnerable then."

Word was quickly sent around the village that people should prepare provisions for the night. Then Tom led them through the woods to the shining shores of the lake.

It looked beautiful in the golden light of the setting sun, hemmed with tall trees that were reflected in the wide, still waters. Looking out over the glowing expanse of water, Tom could almost believe that the lake really did have healing qualities. He certainly hoped so. But even if the lake had no special powers, at least the people were away from the village and perhaps harder for Soltra to track down.

It took a while for the large camp to settle down for the evening. The sun went down and the star-filled night turned the lake silver, but there was no sign of Soltra. Maybe the lake's waters were protecting them.

Small groups of villagers sat around fires, toasting bread and roasting potatoes in the embers.

Sometimes a few voices rose in song, but there was little laughter, and Tom could almost feel the simmering of subdued fear.

Tom and Elenna sat at a fire with Uncle Henry and Aunt Maria. Silver was curled up close to the flames, enjoying the warmth. Storm stood quietly close by.

"So, Tom," Uncle Henry asked, "will you be staying here once you have defeated the Beast?"

Tom shook his head. "I have to find the rest of the golden armor," he said, though he was happy that his uncle had such faith in him. He didn't add that the Dark Wizard had stolen the armor and that a fearsome Beast guarded each piece of it. His aunt and uncle didn't need to know about that. They would only worry.

The fires died down and the villagers prepared for sleep. Soon, only Tom and Elenna and their animal friends were awake.

"I'll take first watch," Tom said to Elenna. "I'll

wake you when I can't keep my eyes open any longer."

Elenna nodded. "Will she come?" she asked.

Tom stared into the trees, knowing that Soltra was out there somewhere.

"I hope she does," he said. "Soltra attacked my home. I must defeat her!"

CHAPTER SIX

THE GIFT

THE LAKE'S WATERS SEEMED TO KEEP SOLTRA at bay. Tom woke ready to take on the Beast. The sun was bright over the treetops and the lakeside camp was bustling. He sprang up. But Aunt Maria stopped him with a gentle hand on his shoulder.

"Do you know what day it is, Tom?" she asked with a smile.

Tom shook his head, puzzled.

Elenna, Storm, and Silver stood nearby. "You didn't tell me!" Elenna grinned.

He stared at her. "What are you talking about?"

"It's your birthday, Tom!" Uncle Henry said. "Did you forget?"

"Is it?" he gasped. So much had happened that he had lost count of the days.

"Yes, it is!" said Elenna. "Happy birthday!"

Silver barked and Storm neighed.

"If things were normal," Aunt Maria said, "we would celebrate properly, but . . ." Her voice trailed away.

"We have more urgent matters to attend to," said Uncle Henry. "We'll celebrate when this is over. Now that it is daylight again, we should return to the village and call a meeting."

"Yes, Uncle Henry, good idea," Tom said.

Elenna pulled him away from the others. "What's the point of that?" she whispered. "They won't be able to do anything to stop Soltra."

"I know," Tom replied softly. "But a village meeting will be the perfect cover for what I have to do. It will keep Uncle Henry and Aunt Maria busy and allow me to slip away unnoticed."

"You mean it will allow *us* to slip away unnoticed," she corrected him.

Tom smiled. He was glad that he had such a brave and loyal friend. "We can't let another night come without confronting the Beast," he told her. "Remember, when she enchanted Farmer Gretlin she had her back to the setting sun. I think she can't stand to have her face toward sunlight. That might be our best weapon. If we can find her and force her into daylight, we may be able to defeat her."

"Farmer Gretlin was in his field near the marsh when he was turned to stone," Elenna said. "So we'll have to start there."

"Yes," Tom replied. "And there's no time to waste. While there's blood in my veins, I'll save my village and defeat Soltra!"

At mid-morning, the villagers gathered for their meeting in the main square. Tom, Elenna, and the two animals stood out of sight behind the forge, getting ready to leave for the marsh.

Tom was pulling on his chain mail when his uncle appeared around the corner.

"You intend to leave the village while we talk," he said, "to find the Beast."

Tom nodded. There was no point trying to lie.

"I understand," Uncle Henry said gently. "But before you go, there is something I want to give you."

"What is it?" Tom asked. He felt proud, wearing the golden chain mail in front of his uncle. It glinted in the morning sunshine.

"It's in the forge," his uncle said. "Your father left it for you."

Tom's eyes widened in amazement; his uncle had never mentioned a gift from his father before. His mind raced as he and Elenna followed Uncle Henry into the forge. What could it be?

"Help me to move the anvil," said Uncle Henry.

Tom grasped one end of the anvil and helped to shift it across the floor. Then his uncle took a spade and began to dig in the hard-packed earth.

Shortly, the spade rang on something hollow. A few moments later, a square wooden box was revealed, about a hand-span in length and depth.

Uncle Henry laid the box on the anvil and undid the metal clasp of the lid.

"It's yours to open," he told Tom.

Tom picked up the box, his thoughts whirling as he wondered what secrets his father's box might contain.

CHAPTER SEVEN

DESTINY AND DANGER

EAGERLY, TOM OPENED THE LID. INSIDE THE box, something lay wrapped in a dark red velvet cloth. He lifted it out. It was heavy and solid. Tom unfolded the velvet wrap and gave a gasp of delight. It was a compass, made of brass and decorated with curling patterns of fine silver.

"It's beautiful," said Elenna. "But I've never seen a compass with such markings."

Engraved on the top of the compass were two words, one at either side of the needle.

"'Destiny,'" Tom read quietly. "And 'Danger.'" He looked up at his uncle. "What does it mean?"

"Turn it over," Uncle Henry said.

On the back were engraved the words: "For My Son."

Tom bit his lip, fighting back tears of joy, as well as regret that he had never known his father. He felt Elenna's calming hand on his shoulder.

"Taladon left this in my keeping when he departed Errinel on his own Quest," said Uncle Henry. "He asked that I give it to you on your first birthday as a hero. That day has come."

Tom looked at his uncle. He could feel his eyes brimming. "Did he leave any message for me?" he asked.

"No," his uncle replied. "But the compass needs no explanation. The needle will show you when to step forward to meet your destiny, and when to flee impossible danger. Your father believed that it would save your life one day."

"Perhaps today," Tom murmured, gazing at the compass. "Thank you." He held the compass tightly; he had never felt so close to his lost father.

Then he gazed out of the doorway of the forge. It was time to go in search of Soltra the Stone Charmer.

Tom, Elenna, Silver, and Storm stood at the edge of the marsh, gazing out over the barren wasteland. Even in the full light of the sun, coils and wreaths of fog drifted and crept low, like evil phantoms seeking their prey.

"Have you ever been in there before?" Elenna asked.

Tom shook his head. "It's too treacherous," he said. "Aunt Maria always told me that only a fool would risk it."

"Or someone very brave," Elenna said.

Tom drew his sword and checked that his shield was securely fastened to his back. He could feel the weight of the compass in his pocket, tucked away under his chain mail. He felt strong in heart, ready for the battle ahead. He had placed the golden helmet safely in Storm's saddlebag.

"How are we going to avoid Soltra's eye?" Elenna asked. Tom could tell from her voice that she was afraid.

"I'll find a way," Tom said.

"*We'll* find a way, you mean."

"No," Tom said firmly. "It's my village. This time I have to do it alone."

Elenna's eyes were determined. "Never!" she said.

Tom shook his head with a rueful smile. Elenna was as strong-willed as he was. "Come on, then," he said. "But watch your footing. The farther we go, the more dangerous the ground will become."

They moved slowly into the tall, whispering reeds, Tom leading Storm, Silver keeping close to Elenna. The fog rose to cover them like a damp blanket. Soon, they came to stretches of black water and had to pick their way along narrow paths of solid ground.

Storm became jittery, his hooves sinking into the soft earth. At last, he neighed and pulled back, bringing Tom to a halt. Tom patted his neck and spoke softly to him, but it was clear the brave stallion would go no farther. Silver crouched low, his ears back and his eyes narrow slits.

"Will you stay back with Storm and Silver?" Tom asked Elenna. "We can't ask them to go any farther, and I don't want to leave them here unprotected."

Elenna nodded, and slotted an arrow to her bow in readiness.

Tom stepped into the fog.

"Remember," he heard her call, "if you're in danger, summon one of the good Beasts of Avantia."

He turned to wave, but already his companions had been swallowed by the fog. He was alone. His hand strayed to the compass tucked under his chain mail and the feel of it gave him comfort.

He squelched onward, his feet sinking into the boggy ground as the pools of stagnant and stinking water began to widen. The fog was so thick now that he could not see the sun above his head. The reeds hissed and quivered.

He paused, breathing in the foul air, staring around. How would he find the Beast in this? She could be close enough to reach out an arm and touch him, and he would hardly know it. Not even the golden helmet could help him see in fog like this. Perhaps the compass could help, but before he had the chance to take it out, a gentle voice spoke out of the fog.

"Welcome to my home."

Tom gripped his sword tightly. "Where are you?" he shouted.

"I am close," said the voice. "Why do you not come and see me?"

Tom had never heard such a beautiful voice before.

He stepped forward, sheathing his sword. "Please?" he whispered, his senses drifting away from him. "Let me see you."

"Come," said the voice. "It is not far."

Tom stumbled on. But suddenly he tripped, lost his balance, and staggered sideways, falling into the tall reeds. His foot plunged into deep slime, and he couldn't pull it out.

With a cry of fear, he found himself knee-deep in thick, oozing mud. He struggled to free himself, but with every movement he sank deeper.

He was trapped!

CHAPTER EIGHT

THE MARSH

THE OOZING MUD SUCKED AT TOM'S LEGS, dragging him slowly deeper, and suddenly he felt as if he had awoken from a dream. Thrashing about would only make it worse, he realized.

"I must not panic," Tom gasped. "I have to keep calm and find a way to pull myself out." He leaned forward and grasped at a tussock of long reeds, but the reeds were slimy and he couldn't get a good grip.

He sank to his waist. How could he have been stupid enough to listen to that voice? Harsh, grating laughter filled his ears. *Malvel!* The evil wizard was mocking him, enjoying his triumph.

He heard Elenna in the distance. "Tom? Are you all right?"

Then there was another voice. "Come to me," sang Soltra's beautiful voice from across the marsh. "Come and stay with me forever."

Tom tried to block out the voice, focusing all his concentration on pulling himself free. But it was hopeless. He gave a howl of anger and despair as the mud rose to his armpits. After all his battles against the Beasts of Avantia, was he going to die in a stinking mud pit?

Then he saw something long and slender come hissing toward him through the fog. It curved downward and hit the mud a few feet away from him. It was an arrow — and tied to the shaft was a rope.

"Elenna!" he gasped. He fought with all his strength to get to the arrow, leaning far over, his fingers stretching out.

Elenna's faint voice called to him. "Tom? Did you get it?"

"Almost!" he shouted. Finally, his fingers closed around the rope. "Yes!"

"Storm will pull you out!" yelled Elenna.

Tom wrapped a loop of rope around his wrist as it tightened. For a few dreadful moments, the mud clung to him. But then, slowly, Tom felt himself being dragged out of the slime. Soon, there was firm earth under his fingers. He scrabbled and kicked with his legs and suddenly he was lying gasping on solid ground. He'd never been so close to death before.

He got to his feet, his legs shaking. "How did you know what to do?" he shouted to Elenna.

"I heard you cry out," she called back. "I fired the arrow toward the sound of your voice. I'm coming!"

"No!" Tom shouted. "Stay back — it's too dangerous." But he knew he needed help. Then he remembered all the good Beasts of Avantia and one in particular: Cypher the Mountain Giant! With his sure footing and ability to destroy mountain mists, he could help Tom through the marsh. Quickly he took his shield from his back and rubbed the center — where a single tear from Cypher had fallen — desperately hoping that it would work.

Almost instantly, he saw a shape coming toward him through the fog. Was it Soltra? Tom raised his mud-smeared shield and gripped the hilt of his sword tightly, ready to draw it once more.

The approaching shape was huge. Soon, it was close enough for Tom to be able to make out its features — the shaggy hair, the shambling gait, and the familiar face peering down at him with its one friendly brown eye.

"Cypher!" Tom gasped with relief.

The giant swung his huge arms, magically whisking away the fog around them. Only then did Tom see a second form standing dark and still in a long robe among the reeds.

"Welcome, Tom," sang the beautiful voice. "Come to me."

Long arms reached out, the robe rippling like black water. Tom stared at her, struggling to keep hold of his senses. But the voice was so lovely, and he could see that Soltra was tall and slender, the oval where her face should have been as smooth as glass and as white as milk, her auburn hair piled in shining rings on her head.

Tom took a step toward her. Cypher let out a roar of warning.

"No, Cypher," Tom whispered, his mind suddenly as white and blank as the fog. "It's all right." He only wanted to be near her.

He stumbled toward Soltra, the fog closing behind him once again. Her great green eye opened. Tom stopped. Then he took another step forward, gazing into the beautiful eye.

→ CHAPTER NINE →

THE GREEN EYE

A TERRIFIED VOICE SHOUTED FROM DEEP within Tom's mind. *Look at the compass!*

Forcing his body to obey, he drew the compass out of his pocket, holding it up in front of his eyes. The needle on the compass pointed to Danger.

"Oh!" he gasped, as the power of Soltra's gaze was broken. His mind clear again, he continued to walk slowly forward, his eyes fixed on the compass. He had to get closer to the Beast if he was to defeat her.

"Come to me," crooned the voice.

Tom was no longer hypnotized by the voice, and the Beast was now only a few strides away. The urge to look into her eye was growing again. His feet faltered and he stood still.

Soltra glided toward him. In one practiced movement, she drew a whip from her cloak and lashed out. Tom heard a hiss as the whip came snaking forward.

He raised his shield, blocking the attack. But before he could strike, Soltra disappeared, swallowed by the fog once again.

How can I fight the Beast when I can't even look at her? Tom wondered.

Tom concentrated, listening closely. Suddenly, he heard soft, cackling laughter from behind. Tom spun around, raising his shield.

He was just in time. The whip thudded against the shield's surface. Soltra's laughter was cut short. This time, Soltra did not disappear into the fog. The whip snapped forward once more, catching Tom around the legs.

He was caught!

Then a roar sounded. It was Cypher! He loomed over Tom, blowing the fog away with the power of his hands and his breath, allowing him to see.

Now Tom could make out the blurry white disk of the sun. Hope rose in him. He stood up and turned to face the Stone Charmer. But as he did so, he foolishly allowed his gaze to rest upon the huge green eye.

A feeling of peace and joy flooded him once again. He smiled, forgetting everything as an icy numbness seeped through his limbs.

"The cold is no danger," crooned Soltra's voice. "Stone is your destiny."

Cypher roared angrily and Malvel's scornful laughter filled Tom's head.

This time it was Malvel's laughter that broke the spell. It filled Tom with determination, and the golden chain mail gave him renewed strength of heart. He tore his eyes from Soltra's face and the ice left his limbs.

"While there is blood in my veins," he shouted, "I will defeat you!"

Cypher gave another roar, once more waving away the fog above Tom's head. Somehow the giant understood that Tom needed the sunlight to defeat Soltra. Golden light filtered down and Soltra was revealed again, but the afternoon sun was behind her now.

"Too late," Soltra sang as she moved forward. "The sun is low, the day is done."

Tom gritted his teeth. If only she could be made to stare into the sun!

Then he had an idea. Hastily Tom put the compass into his pocket and drew his sword. Lifting it above his head, he angled the blade to catch the sunlight on the steel edge. He had to be quick. Soon, he would be within reach of her coiling whip.

Just when he was beginning to lose hope, his blade caught the sun and a burst of golden light was reflected straight into Soltra's eye. She screamed in agony, lunging forward, her long arms reaching for him.

With the last of her strength, Soltra let out a howl and closed her long fingers around Tom's throat, choking him in her frozen grip.

CHAPTER TEN

THE TOUCH OF DEATH

Tom could feel the strength fading from his muscles as he fought for breath. He could do nothing to stop the Beast now.

He was about to lose consciousness when he heard another roar. *Cypher!* The Mountain Giant appeared above him and swung his great arm, striking Soltra so that her grip loosened on Tom's throat.

Tom didn't waste a moment. With a final effort, he raised his sword. He managed to catch the sunlight on his blade once more, and the great green eye was flooded with the brilliant reflection of the sun.

Soltra let out a terrible scream and crumbled into dust, the golden breastplate clanging as it hit the ground.

Panting, Tom stooped to pick it up. The breastplate was decorated with etched muscles, and leather strips with metal buckles secured the sides. He clasped it around himself, threading the strips through the buckles. It fit him perfectly! He flexed his arms, feeling the muscles swell, and understood immediately that the breastplate gave him great physical strength.

He looked up at Cypher. "Thank you!" he called. "I would have failed without your help!"

Cypher gave a roar of delight before turning and loping away, his huge body quickly lost in the fog. Tom knew that the deep bond between him and all the good Beasts of Avantia would never be broken.

Tom turned and ran back through the fog toward where he hoped Elenna, Silver, and Storm would be waiting for him. He longed to be with his friends again.

"Tom?" It was Elenna's voice! "I heard roaring and screaming. Are you all right?"

The shape of his friend, together with Storm and Silver, appeared through the fog.

"Soltra is no more," Tom told them. "And look what she left behind!"

"The next piece of the armor!" Elenna cried in delight. "That's the best birthday present ever! But what was the roaring we heard? It reminded me of Cypher."

"I'll tell you everything on our way back to Errinel," Tom said with a smile.

The villagers greeted Tom and his companions with cheers of joy.

"We were hopeful that you had beaten the Beast when our stone friends and Farmer Gretlin's oxen were returned to life," Uncle Henry said.

The three villagers who had been turned to stone waved at Tom, smiling cheerily.

"It was a close thing," Tom admitted. "My father's compass helped."

"Will you all stay for a while?" asked Aunt Maria. "We have a lot to celebrate!"

"I'm sorry, but we can't," Tom said, giving her a quick hug. "A friend of mine is missing, and I still have work to do for the king."

Uncle Henry stepped forward. "Then go with our blessing," he said. "But return to us as soon as you can."

It was hard to leave Errinel so quickly, but Tom, Elenna, Storm, and Silver were soon on the road away from the village. They would be able to travel a long way before making camp for the night.

"Have you looked at the map?" Elenna asked. "Do we know where we're heading?"

"Not yet," Tom admitted. "I just needed to get out of the village quickly, or I never would have been able to leave." He looked back over his shoulder. "Sometimes battling Beasts is not the hardest part of a quest," he said.

"I understand," Elenna said.

Suddenly, there was a clap of thunder, and forked lightning struck the path ahead of them. Silver whined and Storm neighed in fear.

Malvel! He stood in their way, his arms stretched out so that his cloak was spread wide.

"We're not afraid of you!" Tom shouted, drawing his sword and brandishing it in the air, although he knew he was looking at a vision.

The Dark Wizard smiled and drew one side of his cloak back. "Are you sure?" he asked as a shivering figure was revealed, kneeling on the path.

"Aduro!" Elenna gasped.

It was the good wizard. His red cloak was missing and he looked pale.

"See how I have humbled the great Aduro,"

Malvel crowed. "How long do you think a boy like you can stand against me?"

"Long enough!" Tom shouted. "I'll rescue Aduro!"

"Listen well," snarled Malvel. "You may have won your golden breastplate, but the battle is not over!" The Dark Wizard's eyes flashed. "If you continue your Quest, there will be a heavy price to pay."

Tom glared at him. "What will the price be?" he asked.

"You shall see!" said Malvel. There was another crack of thunder and a flash of lighting, then both wizards were gone.

"What do you think he meant?" Elenna asked, her voice subdued.

Tom looked at her. "I don't know," he said. "But it doesn't matter." He flicked the reins and Storm broke into a trot. "Nothing is going to stop us from fulfilling the Quest. Aduro sent us, and we must complete it in order to rescue him."

Storm raced along the road, Silver loping alongside them as they all headed into a new adventure.

Whatever lay ahead, Tom would defeat it. He had to. This was his destiny.